This book belongs to:

. . . .

to Anne Stones and everybody
at la Petite École Française

Musgrove in

Kensington Gardens

by

Ilona Rodgers

Stacey International

It was a grey October afternoon. Hermione and Musgrove were standing at the window watching the wind blow the leaves around Notting Hill.

"How I hate the autumn half-term!" sighed Musgrove.

"I am bored," moaned Hermione. "I want to go to Princess Diana's playground - to the swings."

"It'll be too cold and windy to go to Kensington Gardens," Musgrove replied. "And I have nothing warm to wear."

Just then the door-bell rang.
"Delivery!" called a cheery voice.
Musgrove went to the door...

... and presently returned with
a rather large parcel.

Attached to the parcel was a note.

$20\frac{21}{X}07$

The Glebe House
Groombridge
Kent

My Darling Nephew,
when I heard about
the cough you had last
winter I got terribly
worried and decided to knit
you a scarf. I gathered up
all my ends of wool and
set to work. Here it is at last.
Your Affectionate
Aunt Aurelia

Musgrove opened the parcel
and began to unfold the scarf.
It went on
and on . . .

... and on and on.

"Your Aunt Aurelia must think you've turned into a giraffe," giggled Hermione.

"Oh dear!" murmured Musgrove.

Musgrove wound the scarf round and around his neck.

"Now we can go out," he announced.

"You can't possibly go dressed like that," protested Hermione.

"I can and I will," declared Musgrove. "It is a present from Aunt Aurelia and out of respect to her I have to wear it. At least once."

Off they went to Princess Diana's Playground in Kensington Gardens. Hermione ran straight up to the swings.

Alas! Because of the half term there was a long queue of children with their nannies, mummies and grannies all on their mobile phones.

"Let's do something else first," suggested Musgrove. "With luck they'll go home soon."

First they went to the Pirate Ship.

Hermione climbed to
the Crow's Nest at
the very top.

Next they went to the Musical Hop-Scotch. While Musgrove searched for conkers, Hermione hopped the tune of Twinkle Twinkle Little Star.

Next they sheltered in their favourite wigwam, for it had started to drizzle with rain.

Musgrove peeked out at the queue for the swings. Despite the rain, the queue wasn't getting any shorter.

"This is ridiculous," grumbled Musgrove. "I am not queuing!"

Suddenly his face lit up. "I've got an idea," he said. "Let's go."

Musgrove led Hermione to a huge plane tree.

"Look after these, please," he said, handing her his bowler, his newspapers and his cane.

He kicked off his galoshes and clambered up the tree to a thick strong branch.

Hermione looked at him in amazement. She had never seen Musgrove do anything like this before.

Balancing precariously, Musgrove
took his scarf off, let one
end down to the ground,
tied the other to the middle
of the branch, and came sliding
down the scarf right into
a pile of old leaves.

Recovering from his landing,
Musgrove shook himself,
picked bits of bark out of his
coat and started to tie a big
fat knot in the end of the scarf.

"Now," said Musgrove to Hermione. "Sit on the knot, cross your legs and hold on tight. Are you ready?"

"Yes!" cried Hermione.

"Are you steady?" asked Musgrove as he drew her back on the scarf.

"Y-e-e-s!" cried Hermione trembling with excitement.

"Go!" said Musgrove. Away she flew.

The scarf swept the ground and soared up and up and up. "I can touch the trees! I can touch the sky! I can touch the rain!" yelled Hermione in delight.

"Particularly the rain," grumbled Musgrove, wiping the inside of his galoshes with a monogrammed handkerchief.

All at once Musgrove felt a tap on his shoulder.

A little voice said: "Sir, sir, please, sir, may we have a go on your swing, sir?"

It was a little boy called George. Behind George was Lucy with her brother Sam and behind them was Adrian with his Baba Nina.

"You'd better wait till Hermione has had enough," said Musgrove firmly.

Soon Musgrove was helping the children up on to the swing and Hermione was giving them a push.

It was growing dark.
They heard the Park
attendant's whistle.

"Let's be off," said Musgrove
"They'll manage on their own."

"What about the scarf?"
worried Hermione.

"Never mind the scarf,"
Musgrove reassured her.
"Aunt Aurelia will be so
pleased to learn that she
has knitted such a good swing."

At the gates they looked back.
The playground swings were empty,
but there was a long queue to
swing on the scarf Aunt Aurelia
knitted from all her ends of wool.

There are other books about Musgrove.
They are called:

Introducing Musgrove, the Nanny of
Notting Hill

Musgrove and Father Christmas

Musgrove and the Easter Eggs

"Musgrove, there's Something in my shoe!"

© Ilona Rodgers 2007
Reprinted 2009

Stacey International
128 Kensington Church Street, London W8 4BH
Tel: +44 (0)207 221 7166   Fax: +44 (0)207 792 9288
E-mail: info@stacey-international.co.uk
Website: www.stacey-international.co.uk

ISBN: 9781905299492